The Mystery of
the Missing Moggie

From the files of Police Dog 99...

Also by Keith Brumpton
A Dinosaur's Book of Dinosaurs (with Roger Dinosaur)
Ig and Tig's Trip to Earth

Also by Rusty
Ten Cats I Hate
Pass the Tennis Ball

The Mystery of the Missing Moggie

From the files of Police Dog 99 . . .

What a <u>dastardly</u> crime!

← secret police file

Keith Brumpton

ORCHARD BOOKS

ORCHARD BOOKS
96 Leonard Street, London EC2A 4RH
Orchard Books Australia
14 Mars Road, Lane Cove, NSW 2066
ISBN 1 85213 438 0 (hardback)
ISBN 1 85213 475 5 (paperback)
First published in Great Britain 1992
First paperback publication 1993
© Keith Brumpton 1992

Printed in Great Britain by
Guernsey Press, C.I.

*This book is dedicated to
Sabine and to Lucja (my dog)*

Contents

Hope I haven't forgotten anything...

Contents

Chapter One

A knock in the night

It all began one snowy night in the middle of winter. Brrr!

Being a sensible sort of a pooch I was inside my kennel when suddenly I heard a

at the door.

"Rusty, it's me!" came a shivery sort of a voice. "Hurry up and get ready, we've a case to solve!" The voice belonged to this man,

P.C. Andy Constable, my assistant.

Every dog in the Police Force has to have an assistant, and I'm no exception. Andy isn't very bright, but he's keen and obedient, so we get along just fine.

C'mon boy, shake a leg...

Andy was very impatient...

I told him to hang on a minute...

... I was busy videoing the late night movie, "Lassie Goes West". (I've seen it before of course, but as my friend Desmond the Dachshund always says, "You can't have too much of a good thing.")

Out in the yard it was as cold as the snow on a walrus's moustache ...

Out in the yard it was as cold as the snow on a walrus's moustache...

"What were you doing in there?" asked Andy gruffly. "You take longer to get ready than my mother!"

"All right, all right," I replied. "No need to get your truncheon in a twist."

He held open the rear door of the police van, and waited for me to get in. I told him I'd rather sit in the front.

"Why can't I ride in the front with you?" I whined.

"Because that's the way things are. You won't change my mind. This is one time when you're not getting your own way."

 "Can we have the siren on?" I asked, when we were driving along the main road. "No we *can't*," spluttered Andy.

"Sirens are only for emergencies."

What a spoilsport!

I took out the street map ready to give Andy some directions.

I pointed out the churchyard on Winkler Street, which is a great place to raise a leg in comfort, but Andy didn't seem interested. He was more worried about Sergeant Brisket.

← Sergeant Brisket

He's our boss at Whistlebridge Police Station, and he's a hard man. So hard he eats Farley's Rusks without milk.

Unfortunately he doesn't like me or Andy. He especially doesn't like me because I'm just a mongrel and he says only Alsatians should be allowed to work in the Police Force. I once gave him one of my favourite old tennis balls and he didn't even say "thanks". That's the sort of character he is.

Anyway, back to the story. We were speeding northwards when our radio crackled into life ...

Whistlebridge to Oscar Bravo Car forty-four, do you read me?

I picked up the radio and growled. Sergeant Brisket was on the other end of the line. He didn't seem to understand what I was saying.

Is that you, Constable Constable? You sound strange. Have you got a cold or something? We should be working on your fitness, lad!

It looked like we were in big trouble! Andy was really worried but I remembered the words of my famous ancestor, Sherlock Bones ...

"After a biscuit things always look brighter"

We'd catch that criminal and show Sergeant Brisket just what we were made of!

Andy asked the Sarge to give us some more details on the case ...

> You're to report to number thirty-three Scratchitt Gardens...There's been some kind of an incident there. Speak to a Miss Alison Hitmarsh. Over and out.

A look of determination came over Andy's face. This is the best place for a look of determination. No use having determined-looking knees, for example!

We changed up to second gear and roared off towards Scratchitt Gardens ...

Chapter Two
Pizzas, tears and vanishing moggies

We arrived there about five minutes later, but it took half-an-hour for Andy to get parked.

He wasn't very good at parking and was terrified of getting any more dents in our bumper.

cracked headlight.

bashed grill.

we had more bumps than a family of camels!

As we stood outside number thirty-three, he gave me a friendly pat on the bonce ...

The door opened to reveal a young girl aged about twelve. She looked as if she'd been crying.

"Good evening, miss," began Andy, his teeth chattering with the cold. "My name is P.C. Constable, and this is my assistant, Police Dog 99. We've had a report of an incident and we'd like to speak to Miss Hitmarsh."

"That's me," sobbed the youngster. "Thank goodness you've come!" We followed her into the lounge and Andy shook the snow off his hat.

Alison explained that her mum was out playing football.

Andy took out his notepad and began writing.

Alison nodded.

"And who exactly *is* this Snuffy character? Might not he be the cause of all the trouble?"

Alison blew her nose and looked at Andy crossly.

Well, _hardly_! Snuffy's my cat and it's him who's been stolen.

Andy had been chewing on his pen and had a big smudge of ink on his upper lip.

"I'm sorry, miss," he said kindly. "It's just that we don't get many, er, cat burglaries ... And it's best to get the paperwork clear at this stage."

Not much happening up here

Worried look

Let's take a look at Andy's notebook, as he talked to Alison ...

WHISTLEBRIDGE 👑 POLICE DEPT.

beat Rusty at draughts this morning. AT LAST !!!

INCIDENT : called to N° 33
~~Scr~~ Scratchitt Gardens.

TIME : Forgot my watch. I think it was about
six o'clock.

DATE : Not sure. I think it was January 31st.
or January 32nd. Not ~~even~~ sure which
(check it out later).

WITNESSES : ~~Only one.~~ ~~Alison~~ ALISON HITMARSH.
Aged 12. Reported that her cat had been
stolen.

DESCRIPTION OF CAT : answers to name of SNUFFY.
Quite tall, black, with some white bits on its
paws. (sounds cute!)

OTHER INFO : Cat never normally left
the house. It didn't like strangers or
dogs.

*Alison?
alisan
alisen.*

WHISTLEBRIDGE ♔ POLICE DEPT.   BROOKSIDE 8.00 video.

<u>info contd.</u> Only Alison and her mother were in the house when it disappeared. * arrange to speak to Alison's mother.

<u>important</u> *

    2 other cats in the neighbourhood have already gone missing (check details with Sgt. Brisket).

    Alison then offered me and Rusty a piece of cake. (very tasty). Fruity flavour.

Interview ended after about ten minutes.
2nd piece of cake followed.

    <u>to do</u> -: get some sausages for tea.
    Ring Sally + see what's on at the Odeon.
    Check local paper ads for a pair of second-hand laces for my boots.

RING MUM. get clean socks.

"Will you be able to find him?" asked Alison, still looking tearful. Andy shrugged his shoulders.

I'm afraid we haven't got much to go on, miss.

"I know he makes Mum sneeze and he pinches food off the table, and sometimes he scratches the wallpaper ... but really he's the cutest cat in the world."

Please don't let anything happen to him!

soggy hankie

I waved a paw in Andy's direction to suggest that we search the rest of the house. There was something about this cat caper that didn't feel right.

Chapter Three

The scene of the crime

open window

Alison's bedroom was pretty untidy. It looked like a launderette that had been hit by a hurricane. She apologised for the mess. "We were searching everywhere for Snuffy." This was the chance I'd been waiting for.

The chance to get on with some REAL police work...

I began sniffing for clues and before you could say "Scooby Doo" I'd discovered one ...

SNIFF

A hair!

I got Andy to pop the hair into a bag so that we could take a look at it later on.

 ← the hair in question.

I noticed the window was open. Perhaps this would be an open and shut case after all.

Unfortunately there was no sign of any cat-burglar or even of any cat.

Not even a set of prints in the snow ...

Andy asked if Snuffy might have jumped out of the window.

Alison shook her head. "Snuffy would never do that. He can't stand heights!"

I couldn't believe my ears. What kind of a moggie was that? Nine lives and still a scaredy-cat!

As long as I live, I'll never understand cats ...

But back to the ←case

The long arm of the law.

We were just about to leave the room when Andy spotted something on the drainpipe. A set of fingerprints! He asked Alison if she knew anyone who'd recently shinned up the drainpipe. Not surprisingly, she didn't. Apparently Mr Formby, the window cleaner, used ladders.

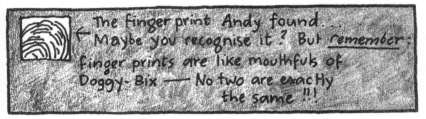

The finger print Andy found.
← Maybe you recognise it? But *remember* :
finger prints are like mouthfuls of
Doggy-Bix — No two are exactly
the same !!!

Alison gave us a photograph of Snuffy to help with our enquiries. I couldn't recall ever having

Snuffy →

chased him up any trees. But then all cats look the same to me, especially when they're hiding underneath Mrs Watson's Mini Metro ...

We left Alison's bedroom with our clues—
1. A hair (owner unknown)

27

2. A set of fingerprints (owner unknown)
3. And a picture of Snuffy (developed at Boots)
It wasn't much to go on!
Especially when we still had

just waiting for us to make a mistake!

At the top of the stairs I suddenly froze and pinned back my ears ...

There was someone downstairs, and from the smell of it they were carrying a fish! Can you guess who it might be and why they might be carrying a fish?

I'm sorry I haven't a clue.

Chapter Four

A fishy character

This was a job for highly trained police officers! I told Alison to stay in her bedroom while we investigated. A floorboard went creak under my front paw ... I felt very frightened. What if the cat-burglar had returned and decided to pinch a dog instead?

With shaking paws I watched as Andy crept downstairs. There was a huge shadow ahead of him!

"That you, Alison?" asked a gruff voice. I peeped round from behind Andy's trouser-leg and saw a large woman standing downstairs.

She was dressed in a brand-new football strip and eating a packet of fish and chips. It was Mrs Hitmarsh, Alison's mum.

"Who are you?" she snapped, fixing poor Andy with an icy gaze.

"Er, it's P.C. Constable here, and Police Dog 99."

She chomped on a chip.

Police dog, eh? He looks more like an advert for the cat and dog shelter. What happened? Did you run out of Alsatians?

What a cheek! I wanted to tell her that I had passed all my exams, that I was top of my class, that I could fetch a ball faster than any dog in Whistlebridge ...

Unfortunately Andy had already begun to question her over Snuffy's disappearance.

She didn't seem very interested in her daughter's missing cat and kept talking about the football match instead. Apparently she had scored two goals, then got sent off for foul play. She certainly looked a bit of a bruiser!

"Aren't you worried about your daughter's cat?" persisted Andy.

Mrs Hitmarsh was demolishing a buttie, and replied with a mouthful of chips:

WARNING! →
Don't look at this pic if you've just had your tea!

"No, not really. Cats can look after themselves. They're not as dim as dogs. Anyway, it'll be good to have this house fluff-free for a while."

Alison gave a little whimper.

"I'm sorry," continued Mrs H., "but sometimes you have to be cruel to be kind."

Mrs Hitmarsh didn't look very kind to me. She certainly wasn't shedding any tears over poor Snuffy.

And if she's just played football how come she isn't even muddy?

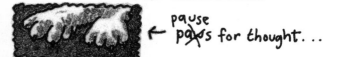

pause
← paws for thought. . .

Andy asked Alison if Snuffy had had any enemies. She sat down next to her goal-scoring battleaxe of a mum.

"I don't think so."

"Only Mr Scott the milkman. He's always complaining about Snuffy knocking over his bottles to get at the cream," added Mrs Hitmarsh. "Now why don't you leave us in peace! I want to take a shower."

And Alison has homework to do!

Mrs H. was about as talkative as a tin of salmon.

Andy wrote down Mr Scott's address at the dairy

Shed number 3
Whistlebridge Dairies,
Cowgate Road.

and asked if there was anyone else in the street who knew Snuffy well.

Alison shook her head. "Not really. Like I said,

33

he didn't go out much. You could try Mrs Blixen from the pet shop next door."

I wouldn't go bothering poor Mrs. Blixen. Just give that milkman a good grilling.

Mrs Hitmarsh finished the last piece of her fish supper without even offering me a piece. She got up and looked down on Andy and me.

"Let me show you to the door."

"Yes, of course," stuttered Andy. "Thanks for your help. We'll be back in touch if we hear anything."

The front door slammed behind us,

 and a snowflake landed on my snout.

"Well," said Andy, searching for the keys to the van. "We've got no shortage of suspects. D'you want to look at my list?"

He showed me his notepad.

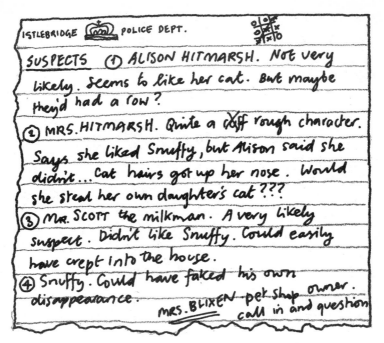

When we were safely inside the van, Andy switched on the heater and we shared a teacake his mum had packed.

Chapter Five

A chapter for which I can't think of a title

Next door to the Hitmarsh home.

Blixen's Pet Shop was very dark and although there was no sign of anyone about,

the front door wasn't locked, so we went inside . . .

Whilst Andy went to look for Mrs Blixen I started to explore on my own. It was a pretty creepy place, with lots of rats scurrying about everywhere.

In the pet shop I made some interesting discoveries.

mmm...

A pile of empty sacks...

counter

A football programme...

January 29th 7.30
WHISTLEBRIDGE
LADIES F.C.
v
Tiger Bay Belles

And a chip!

Just then someone

switched on the lights

It was Mrs Blixen, and she sounded about as friendly as a charging rhino.

"Yah, can I help?" she asked, without sounding at all helpful. She was another powerful-looking woman, about the same height as Andy, but with more muscles. Andy introduced himself.

Mrs Blixen looked down on me from behind her dark glasses.

At first Andy didn't know what she was on about. "Pardon?" he replied.

"I said my limit is a tenner for the mutt. I can give you ten pounds, but no more. Most people these days want a puppy. Or a pedigree ... And he certainly isn't pedigree, is he?"

Andy was very annoyed. So was I!

"I haven't brought him here to sell! This is my assistant, Police Dog 99!"

Ten pounds indeed! You can't buy a squeaky toy for that these days, let alone a highly trained canine!

Mrs Blixen didn't seem at all bothered by her mistake. In fact she made another joke about trading me in for an Alsatian. She was heading for one of my fiercest growls if she kept this up.

Andy took out his notepad and began asking questions about poor Snuffy.

Mrs Blixen wasn't very helpful. She said she wanted to lock up the shop if we didn't mind buzzing off.

I don't expect you have a search warrant?!!

"I'm just a poor pet shop girl trying to make a living, so go on ... get lost!"

Sergeant Brisket must have been laughing into his mug of hot chocolate.

On the way home in the van we discussed Mrs Blixen. I said that for a pet shop owner she didn't seem to know very much about animals.

"What makes you say that?" asked Andy.

"She had an exercise wheel in the snake's cage!"

Andy wondered if Mr Scott the milkman might still be at the dairy.

"Not unless the cows are on night shift," I joked.

Andy suggested we took a look anyway.

The snow had made the road slippery...

Andy was finding it hard to get a grip.

Sometimes I wish I could take the wheel...

With so much snow about it wasn't easy to find our way!

Chapter Six
Scary Dairy

The siren was wailing as we screeched to a halt in front of Whistlebridge Dairies.

"I told you not to use the siren unless it's an emergency," scolded Andy.

My tail drooped, guiltily.

The yard was all covered with snow, and there were four or five empty milk floats parked by a large shed. Over by the shed door, a lonely figure was locking up for the night.

"Mr Scott?" asked Andy, hoping that this was our suspect.

The man looked nervous.

Andy explained that we weren't interested in his milk float, only a missing cat.

suspect
name: Joseph Scott
height: short!
Hair: brown, badly cut.
Other features: unshaven, one missing tooth, shifty eyes.
Notes: Very nervous. Kept shuffling about. Looked quite a tough nut. definitely doesn't like cats!
birthsign: Taurus.

Mr Scott looked very guilty. Especially when we told him the cat was called Snuffy.

"I never laid a finger on him. He's nothing but trouble, that cat, you ask anybody ... He's a milk-thief and a vandal. What about that? Isn't stealing the cream a crime?"

"Er ... " answered Andy.

I have to pay for every bottle he breaks. The money comes out of my pocket...

"If you ask me you should arrest that kid, Alison. She probably got bored with the cat and flogged it to the pet shop next door."

"Mmm. We hadn't thought of that ... "

Before we left the dairy Andy remembered another important question for Mr Scott.

"Can we have a carton of semi-skimmed milk, please?"

the SUSPECTS SO FAR

Have you got any ideas yet about whodunnit?

Mrs. Hitmarsh?

Alison Hitmarsh?

Snuffy?

Mrs. Blixen?

Mr. Scott? →

Chapter Seven
A troubled morning at
Whistlebridge Police Station

For some reason my alarm clock didn't go off next morning, so we arrived late at the station. I'd been up half the night chewing over the case. And on an old bone.

Now Andy was worried in case we bumped into Sergeant Brisket.

The Sarge hates anyone to be late.

Some more things the Sarge hates —
1. Long hair
2. Shoes that aren't shiny
3. Dogs (except Alsatians)
4. Criminals & unsolved crimes
5. Small portions of nosh

Unfortunately he caught us half way down the corridor and dragged us into his office for a long talk about how important it was always to be on time.

"And you look like a cleaner's mop!" he growled. "You never see my Alsatians with so much as a hair out of place. I said this would happen ... letting strays and mongrels into the force ... "

Rusty's shaping up really well, sir. I'll keep an eye on his appearance in future.

Sergeant Brisket didn't seem very impressed. He said he wouldn't trust Andy to keep watch over a dozing hamster.

Then he asked if we'd made any progress in the cat-burglary case.

Andy told him we were following a few leads.

We went to the canteen for coffee and a bowl of water. What could we do to get to the bottom of this mystery?

Andy was busy talking to his girlfriend.

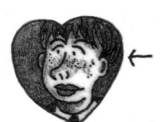

This is her. She's called Sally Swancourt and she's a W.P.C.

Meanwhile I had a quick chat with an old friend of mine, Rex Shepherd. Rex is a very experienced Police Dog and was able to give me a few useful tips.

REX →

Big ears (Useful for listening to station gossip).

Big eyes. (Useful for spotting clues).

Big teeth. (Useful for just about everything)!

Always remember, Rusty, that _everyone_ is a suspect, no matter _who_ they are. Rule nobody out.

Secondly, use every scrap of evidence you have, no matter how small...

I've known cases to turn on a toe-nail. Use the police laboratory to check things out...

And lastly, see if you can find out more about your suspects. Are you any good with computers?

Chapter Eight

Now we're getting somewhere. Aren't we?

I hate computers! Horrible things. And it's very difficult to use the keyboard if you've got paws.

In the end I had to get Andy to operate it for me.

"What is it you want to know?" he asked.

"I want some background info on the suspects. I'd like to know if any of them have got records."

Mrs. Hitmarsh had a C.D. player.

"I meant a *criminal* record!"

Andy began working on the computer. He was pretty sure that Mrs Blixen had nothing to do with the kidnap. He thought Mr Scott the milkman was the likeliest villain.

What do you think?

Thirty minutes later, Andy was still trying to work the computer. "I'm sure I've followed all the instructions correctly, but this is the only information I can get ... "

Latest holiday News		
Resort	Duration	Flt
SPAIN	7 nights	Heathrow
SPAIN	14 nights	Glasgow
JAMAICA	7 nights	Mnchstr

The computer was displaying some details about a holiday in Spain. Seven nights for £235. If Sergeant Brisket had shown up then, we would have been in big trouble.

Oh well, looks like we'll have to rely on good old-fashioned police work. ..So much for computers!

Andy took off his glasses and rubbed his eyes.
"Sorry, old pooch, looks like I let you down."
I gave Andy a lick on the hand. "Don't worry about it, partner, I've still got a few tricks left up my collar."

"I hope so. Otherwise we're in deep trouble. If we don't solve this case we'll be looking for a new job!"

Just then there was a

KNOCK!

at the door. A young policewoman came in.

Andy asked what a forensic test was. The W.P.C. explained that it was a test scientists did to find out information about everyday objects, like the hair we found at Alison's house ...

Andy started to read the report.

"Was it a hamster hair we found?" I asked.

"It was," answered Andy, obviously impressed. "How did you know that?"

This was a very important clue indeed! It would help us to find the phantom catnapper. And if we could do that, Sergeant Brisket would have to let us stay on ...

Andy was crouched behind a hedge with a pair of binoculars and a teacake.

"This is very exciting," he babbled. "It's my first stakeout." I wished he'd stop mentioning steak . . . It was making me hungry!

"Have a piece of teacake," he offered.

It was a freezing cold night and overhead hundreds of stars were shining like the lights on a Christmas tree.

Andy blew on his fingers to try and keep them warm. He asked who we were looking out for.

"We're in Scratchitt Gardens," I growled. "Surely you can guess?"

"Not Mrs Blixen, surely?" he exclaimed. "I've told you it wasn't her. She likes animals."

Just then we heard a door

on the other side of the street. Andy grabbed his
binoculars.

"There's someone coming out of Blixen's Pet
Shop ... He's carrying something."

"What?" I asked.

"It looks like an old sack."

I wagged my tail ... ... This was just
as I had hoped.

"What now?" asked Andy, as baffled as ever.
He was as lost as a bone in a very large garden.

"That's our suspect off to kidnap a few more helpless moggies . . .

worried puss → Oh no!

He'll be back later. All we can do until then is wait. Sherlock Bones used to pass the time by playing his violin. I don't suppose you have one on you?"

Sorry, just my recorder.

I didn't fancy listening to Andy playing "Three Blind Mice" on his recorder, so I put on my headphones and began howling along to a favourite tape.

Like most dogs I'm into HEAVY METAL. Something you can really tap your paws to!

The tape had long since finished and I was curled up, fast asleep, when Andy began shaking me.

What a sight to wake up to!

"Hey, boy! You were right ... Wake up! He's back!"

In the distance we could see a large dark figure outside the pet shop.
He had a sack
over his shoulder.
A bulging sack.

"What next?" asked Andy.

"We arrest him of course, for the kidnap of Snuffy the cat."

We ran towards the sinister catnapper, and Andy shouted out:

"Stay right where you are!"

If only Sergeant Brisket could see us now, in action at last!

Chapter Ten
The big chase scene

The villain didn't hang around waiting to be caught. As soon as he saw me running towards him he started to shin up the nearest drainpipe.

Bits of plaster dropped down on to my bonce, and in a flash the hooded figure was up on the roof and out of sight. Andy arrived, breathless.

"Did you see his face?" he puffed.

I shook my head.

"Well, what are you waiting for, Rusty? After him!"

I didn't much fancy using that old drainpipe. It looked dangerous. I decided to use the fire escape instead.

The villain shouted down from the roof in a strange muffled voice:

He was still shouting down at Andy when I appeared at the top of the fire escape!

Unfortunately the manic moggie molester heard me, and spun round on his giant wellies ...

I asked him to come quietly, like a good villain, but he didn't budge. Not even a centimetre.

Before I could say anything the mad catnapper produced a large snake from the inside of his coat. It began to HISS. (The snake, not the coat!)

Isn't this hiss-terical ??

"Ever seen a boa constrictor before?" asked the villain, with a cruel laugh. My tail drooped.

" ... And this one hasn't had any tea today, have you, Betty?"

Betty the snake moved forward menacingly, her forked tongue flicking out from time to time. She had a very hungry look in her beady little eyes.

Fancy a quick cuddle?

I was an extremely worried Police Dog, but I tried to keep calm and to remember my training. Andy had just appeared on the roof beside me, and seeing him gave me an idea.

I asked if he still had his recorder. He reached inside his uniform.

"Then how about playing some music for our slithery chum over there?" I suggested.

Andy put the recorder to his lips and blew, nervously. He began to play an old snake-charming tune.

the tune Andy played

Almost immediately, Betty the boa constrictor began to sway from side to side. Gradually she coiled herself into a ball and went to sleep ...

Chapter Eleven
Truth and proof on the roof

The catnapper was furious.

Betty! Betty! Wake up!

he shouted. "Don't let me down now, you ungrateful serpent! When I think of all the mice I've given you!"

I looked up at the catnapper and barked a happy bark . . .

How many snake owners do we know?

only one..

MRS. BLIXEN !!!

"Yes! That's right," laughed the hooded figure, moving backwards towards the fire escape. "I am the phantom catnapper of Whistlebridge. And I haven't finished yet!

... The last ones in the neighbourhood ... I have over fifty in my cellar, ready to be sent abroad."

"Why??? Poor dog! Not very bright, are you? I hate cats, that's why! They give me an allergy. Runny nose, red eyes. I hate their fat chubby bodies, their droopy whiskers, their funny smells ... And hairs everywhere ... I CAN'T STAND THE SIGHT OF THEM!"

"I know a carpet manufacturer who will take the cats off me for a good price. They should make a nice rug or two. And then Whistlebridge will be cat-free for all time!"

Mrs Blixen made a run for the fire escape, but I was after her. Before she could reach the steps I bounded forward and stood there growling. I must have looked pretty fierce because she put her hands up and called out to Andy:

Andy was just about to put the cuffs on Mrs Blixen when a gust of wind blew off her hood, and sent her dark glasses spinning to the ground. Then a second later, her wig blew off too ... up into the sky, leaving Mrs Blixen exposed for all the world to see ...

Mrs Blixen was Mrs HITMARSH!!! Alison's soccer-mad mum and the cat-napping pet shop owner were none

Mrs. Blixen becomes Mrs. Hitmarsh!

other than the same person!

Well knock me down with a squeaky toy.

Andy read the list of charges and told Mrs Hitmarsh her rights.

OK, OK, we've all seen 'The Bill'. Let's get off this roof, it's freezing!

"A few years ago, when I first came to Whistle-bridge, I worked in Blixen's Pet Shop for the real Mrs Blixen. The only trouble was she kept loads of cats and I had my allergy ... my life was a misery. Always sneezing and wheezing, itchy eyes and streaming hooter ...

> I've got a wet nose too, but I don't mind.

"I told Mrs Blixen, 'Either the cats go or I go,' and would you believe it, she chose to get rid of me! Gave me the sack! She chose to keep those rotten tabbies instead! Left me without a job, and with a kid to look after. And then, would you believe it, she brought a kitten round for Alison's birthday!

> That was Snuffy. Made matters even worse, he did, because Alison thought the little blighter was cute and wouldn't let me get rid of him. My life was a misery with all those cats about!

Years of sneezing lay ahead, until one night I was eating my pizza and I thought to myself, 'Why put up with all this? Get rid of the cats and you get rid of the problem!'

I decided to catch all the cats one by one, and to smuggle them abroad for a good price.

So why did you disguise yourself as Mrs. Blixen?

"Because if anyone saw me, I wanted her to get the blame. It's all her fault anyway. Her and those rotten cats. At least in prison it should be cat-free. Now can we get off this roof before I freeze to death?"

I pointed my paw towards the fire escape.

Just as we were leaving we heard a mewing sound. Andy went over to Mrs Hitmarsh's sack and lifted out a couple of worried-looking kittens.

It's OK now. You've nothing to worry about. Nothing at all . . .

Chapter Twelve

The case against...

I managed to put my paws on the following evidence –

1. The hamster hair found in Alison's bedroom.

Of all the people we interviewed, only the false Mrs Blixen had a hamster (in the pet shop).
The hair must have come off her clothing when she shinned up the drainpipe to snatch Snuffy.

2. The sacks behind the counter in the pet shop. Perfect for carrying petrified tabbies!

3. The prints on the drainpipe matched Mrs Hitmarsh's mitts.

BUT!

Finger print

Fish finger print

I never guessed that Mrs Hitmarsh had been impersonating Mrs Blixen.
I missed the clue of the football programme in the pet shop

(Of course, Mrs. Hitmarsh played football for Whistlebridge Ladies F.C.)

They looked and smelled so similar, how could I have been fooled by that old wig?!

Never mind, even Lassie the Wonderdog makes the odd mistake!

"Very clever," snarled Mrs Hitmarsh to Andy as we sat in the van. "Stick with this mutt and you could make it to C.I.D."

Back at the Police Station we bumped into Sergeant Brisket again.

He was looking annoyed because he'd seen me riding in the front seat of the van. Andy wasn't worried. He explained that I'd had to sit in the front because we had a dangerous criminal in the back.

dangerous criminal.

dangerous sergeant.

He told Sergeant Brisket all about Mrs Hit-marsh and how we'd cracked the case.

"These two are smart," added the handcuffed Mrs H . . .

They should be PROMOTED !!!

Sergeant Brisket nodded. "Yes, well, good work Constable, and, er, you too, dog." He bent down to pat me on the head!!!

We handed Mrs Hitmarsh over to the custody officer and got changed ready to go home.

On the way out we saw a very pale-looking Sergeant Brisket sitting in a chair, all-a-tremble. He was as white as a tin of Dulux Extra White.

One of Andy's friends explained that the Sarge had opened one of Mrs Hitmarsh's sacks, the one containing Betty, the boa constrictor!

evening all !

Chapter Thirteen.

Time to put my paws up

That night we celebrated our success. We had a hot fire, a place in front of the TV, and a bowl of chocolate popcorn. Andy was sitting on the sofa, next to his girlfriend, W.P.C. Sally Swancourt.

Sally suggested that we play catch. I wagged my tail in agreement, but Andy didn't look too happy. He always finishes last when we play catch. I think it's because he keeps trying to catch the ball in his hands instead of using his mouth like me!

"What happened to Mrs Hitmarsh?" I hear you ask. Well, she went on trial and the judge gave her two years in prison. She wasn't very happy, poor woman. She said she wanted at least ten.

The real Mrs Blixen turned out to be on safari in Iceland (apparently she didn't see a single giraffe!). She came back last week and now Blixen's Pet Shop is open for business as usual, so if you want to buy a tabby yourself, you know the address.

We found Snuffy, and all the other cats, safe and sound. Snuffy and Alison have gone to live with their Aunty Mildred in a pleasant street on the west side of Whistlebridge, just next to the old railway line.

So now there are plenty of cats to chase again. Looks like I'll have to get back into shape ...

WARNING: This is the ~~last~~ second page of this book. Please observe safety procedures when closing.

Thank you.

SAFE BOOK SOCIETY

About the authors

Keith Brumpton was one of Britain's most promising young gymnasts until a fall from his pram at the age of two ended his career. After his parents moved to Peru (to try and get away from him), Keith befriended a colony of bears living deep in the forests of the Ukraine, and stayed there for twelve years. He now has a small barge on the Rochdale canal and a large bump on his left leg.

Rusty Barker was one of a litter of six pups, born and raised in Whistlebridge. He studied tennis balls in the local park, and went on to specialize in wrestling with sticks. He likes watching TV, shredding copies of the *Radio Times* and sitting in chairs he's not supposed to.